For Mallory Loehr,
who believes in imaginary things
in a way so rare & true
—E.W.M.

Copyright © 2020 by Emily Winfield Martin

All rights reserved. Published in the United States by
Random House Children's Books,
a division of Penguin Random House LLC, New York.

Random House and the colophon are registered trademarks of
Penguin Random House LLC.

Visit us on the Web! rhcbooks.com

Educators and librarians, for a variety of teaching tools,
visit us at RHTeachersLibrarians.com

Library of Congress Cataloging-in-Publication Data is available upon request.
ISBN 978-0-553-51103-1 (trade)—ISBN 978-0-375-97432-8 (lib. bdg.)—
ISBN 978-0-553-51104-8 (ebook)

The artist used acrylic on wood and gouache on paper
to create the illustrations for this book.
The text of this book is set in 14-point Cochin and hand lettered.

Interior design by Nicole de las Heras

MANUFACTURED IN CHINA
10 9 8 7 6 5 4 3 2 1
First Edition

The
IMAGINARIES

Little Scraps of Larger Stories

Emily Winfield Martin

Random House New York

To the one who finds this,

I don't know where they come from, these scraps, these strings of words, like flickers of a dream: places, creatures, names, characters, mysteries.

All I really know is what I made with them over the years, these strange pictures—fragments of a secret world—illustrations for stories that do not exist.

Imaginary stories. Imaginaries.

I found them, or maybe they found me.

I found one in a lighthouse, one in a packet of seeds, one in the trunk of a hollow tree.

There was one tucked in the corner of a forgotten diorama, one hidden like a pearl in an oyster shell . . . one forgotten in a paperback from a used bookstore in Paris.

I found one pinned to a scrap of silk and one rolled up in a map of stars, one tangled in my headphone cords, one in the roots of an English rose.

I found them in the city when I first lived alone, and in the woods when I was a little girl.

They have come in green glass bottles and in the pocket of an old wool coat. . . .

Now *you* have found them. My Imaginaries. Or did they find you?

Yours truly,

Emily Winfield Martin

Where
they were going,
there were no
maps.

THE
SEA
GIVES
UP
ITS
SECRETS
SLOWLY.

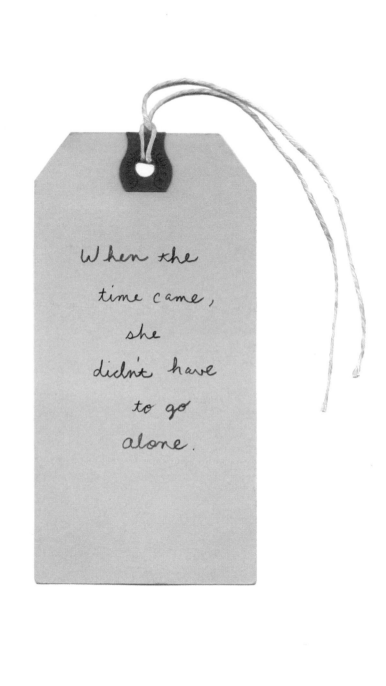

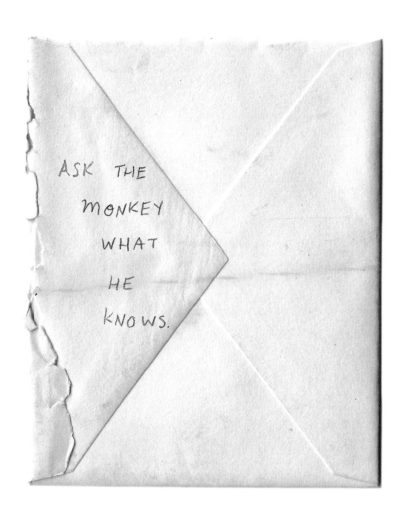

Her

heart was the

kind that beat

like a bird's

wings.

Genevieve
preferred
a crown of
flowers
to a crown of
gold.

The paradise was different
depending on who
found it.

THE
FUTURE
IS A
RUMOR
THE
PAST
TOLD
THE
PRESENT.

Each thought
it was
the other's
fault.

ESME ALWAYS
FOUND SOMETHING
NEW AT
HER
GRANDMOTHER'S
HOUSE.

They had been telling each other stories since they were small.

They
were
shy
in the day...

. . . and fearless
            in the night.

32636

She always wanted
to be
a bear.

Lulu didn't think her friends had come to the party.

The
museum
didn't
Know which
one was
Magic.

She had
a
way
of
setting

things

aglow.

Leonard's
mother was
a snake
charmer.

The
forest
was
especially
enchanted.

She grew
dahlias

the size of
dinner plates.

ONCE
EVERY
ONE
HUNDRED
YEARS,
SOMEONE
IS
BORN
WHO
SPEAKS
CAT.

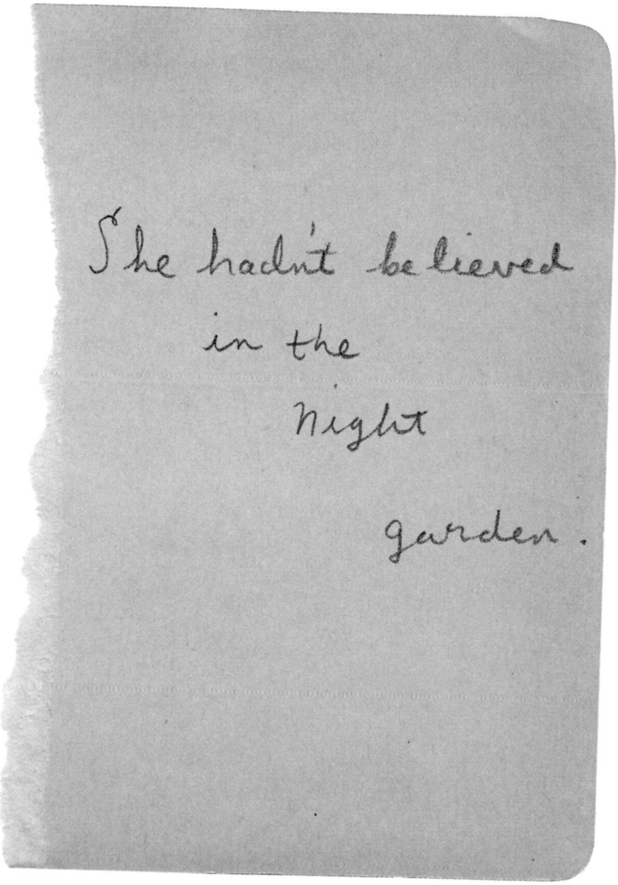

She hadn't believed
in the
night
garden.

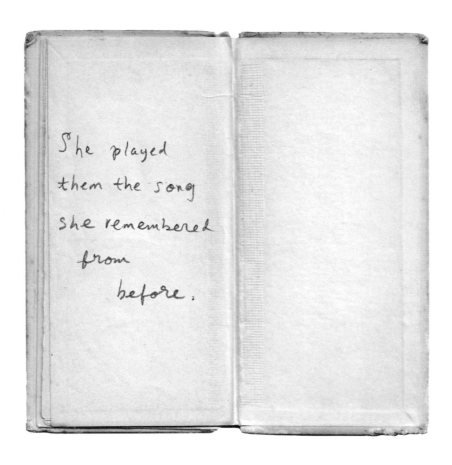

She played
them the song
she remembered
from
    before.

He preferred mischief to magic.

The Sea Monster knew they would ~~never~~ meet again.

THE
MOON
ALWAYS
LISTENS.

THEIR

UNCLE ALWAYS
TOLD THEM HE HAD
LOST HIS EYE
TO LOVE.

Not all libraries are quiet.

Lily wanted
to be
a
good
place
to

land.

HE CAME FROM
AN ANCIENT FAMILY
OF ELEPHANTS.

А. К. Саврасов (1830—1897).
Просека в сосновом лесу. 1883 г.
Государственный Русский музей.
A. K. Savrasov (1830—1897)
An Opening in a Pine Forest. 1883
State Russian Museum

9-894-60 г. Т. 75 000. З 591 Ц. 25 к.
С. 1. 1. 1961 г. и. 3 к.
Московская типография № 2 Мосгорсовнархоза

She
never
told
anyone
what
she
saw
at
the
edge
of
the
world.

From the Author

Before I ever made books, I used to say my paintings were "illustrations for stories that didn't exist." And that's what this book has become home to, on scraps of paper ephemera found haunting treasure-box antique shops, my misfit collection of recurring themes and obsessions: wistful girls and willful girls, flowers, disguises, enchanted creatures, the sea.

It chronicles, more than anything else, the process of someone becoming herself, in the way that we are always becoming more ourselves. I circle back on images and ideas again and again, always building more of the world I've made to live in, to dream in.

And you're invited too, of course you are.

I made it for both of us.

- - - - -

Emily Winfield Martin is a painter of real and imaginary things and the author and illustrator of books like *Snow & Rose* and *The Wonderful Things You Will Be*.

Emily lives in Portland, Oregon, and can often be found tending her garden and watching the waves for sea monsters.

Visit her online at emilywinfieldmartin.com.